What is Indiana Jones doing in Vienna in March 1917?

He's disguised as an Austrian army officer, trying to smuggle a letter back to France . . . a letter that could bring an end to the terrible Great War.

He's met the two people in power who can give him what he needs—but mysterious strangers are out to stop him!

Watch Indy dodge the villains . . . try to change the course of history . . . and continue his quest for lifelong adventure!

Catch the whole story of Young Indy's travels on the amazing fact-and-fiction television series *The Young Indiana Jones Chronicles!*

THE YOUNG INDIANA JONES CHRONICLES
(novels based on the television series)

TV-1. The Mummy's Curse

TV-2. Field of Death

TV-3. Safari Sleuth

TV-4. The Secret Peace

Forthcoming

TV-5. Trek of Doom

TV-6. Revolution!

YOUNG INDIANA JONES BOOKS
(original novels)

Young Indiana Jones and the . . .

1. Plantation Treasure

2. Tomb of Terror

3. Circle of Death

4. Secret City

5. Princess of Peril

6. Gypsy Revenge

7. Ghostly Riders

8. Curse of the Ruby Cross

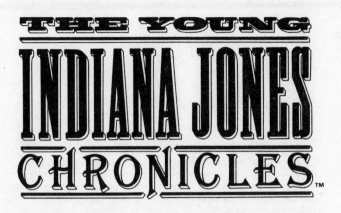

THE YOUNG INDIANA JONES CHRONICLES™

The Secret Peace

Adapted by William McCay

Based on the teleplay "Austria, March 1917"
by Frank Darabont

Story by George Lucas

Directed by Vic Armstrong

With photographs from the television show

RANDOM HOUSE 🏠 NEW YORK

This is a work of fiction. While Young Indiana Jones is portrayed as taking part in historical events and meeting real figures from history, many of the characters in the story, as well as the situations and scenes, have been invented. In addition, where real historical figures and events are described, in some cases the chronology and historical facts have been altered for dramatic effect.

PHOTO CREDITS: Cover and interior photographs by Jaromir Komarek, © 1992 by Lucasfilm Ltd. Map by Alfred Giuliani.

Library of Congress Cataloging-in-Publication Data
McCay, William.
The secret peace / adapted by William McCay ; teleplay by Frank Darabont ; story by George Lucas ; directed by Vic Armstrong.
p.   cm. — (The Young Indiana Jones chronicles ; TV-4)
"Based on the television episode Vienna, March 1917, with photographs from the show."
Includes bibliographical references (p.   ).
Summary: While serving as a special agent in the Belgian army during World War I, seventeen-year-old Indiana Jones accompanies two Bourbon princes on a dangerous secret mission to Austria to try to end the war.
ISBN 0-679-82777-3 (pbk.)
[1. World War, 1914–1918—Austria—Fiction. 2. Spies—Fiction.
3. Adventure and adventurers—Fiction.] I. Darabont, Frank.
II. Lucas, George. III. Armstrong, Vic. IV. Title. V. Series.
PZ7.M129Se   1992   [Fic]—dc20   91-58100

Manufactured in the United States of America   10 9 8 7 6 5 4 3 2 1

The Secret Peace

INDY'S TERRITORY IN "VIENNA, MARCH 1917"

Chapter 1

Young Indiana Jones pedaled his bicycle with an anxious eye on the threatening clouds above. The cobblestone street gleamed with rainwater, and he knew it could start pouring again.

His breath steamed as he pedaled, condensing on his shiny yellow rain slicker. "Everyone says you've got to see April in Paris." Indy shook his head as he glided beneath a row of leafless trees, which dripped down on him. "But they never mention how lousy March can be."

A rumble from the horizon didn't speed his

pedaling. Indy knew it wasn't thunder. It was the dull, rolling crash of artillery fire some fifty miles north of the French capital.

"Who'd have thought that a political assassination would have gotten so many countries at each other's throats?" Indy muttered.

Ever since the Germans invaded two and a half years ago, French troops and their British allies had struggled to keep them at bay. The Germans had also slashed their way through Belgium, though that tiny country had amazed the world by putting up a fight. In search of adventure, Indy had joined the Belgian army and risen through the ranks. Under his slicker, he wore the uniform of a Belgian captain. But despite his officer's status, he was just one more cog in a gigantic military machine.

From the Alps to the English Channel, soldiers faced off in four hundred miles of trenches. And in the battles to date, more than three and a half million of those soldiers had become casualties. That was almost two men for every foot along the front lines.

"Not surprising," Indy said to himself, "when generals were still sending men off in straight lines to get mowed down by machine guns."

More rumbles came—proof of a serious bombardment. Indy wondered if the theory he'd heard lately was true. Had the vibration of all the cannon fire caused the terrible rains since the war had begun? Between the pounding artillery and the rain, the no-man's-land between trenches had turned into a sea of mud. Indy had heard of wounded men sucked helplessly down to drown.

Shuddering, he rounded a corner, pedaled for a block, then coasted up to the building he wanted: the headquarters of French military intelligence. It was a white stone mansion, surrounded by a fence that looked like a parade of cast-iron spears.

Inside, French soldiers patrolled what had once been gardens. Slickers covered their horizon-blue greatcoats. But their distinctive helmets, with the small crest—and their rifles—revealed them as guards.

Even though they were stuck standing in the rain, Indy suspected that the soldiers were happy to be in Paris, rather than on the front lines. Out in the trenches, they'd probably be up to their knees in muddy slime. And there was always the danger of a passing shell burying them in the muck.

Indy had to admit to himself that *he* was glad

to be in Paris. After spending months in the colonial military campaigns in Africa, he was eager to move from the sidelines and back to the crucial front of the war.

Paris was the hub around which all the Allied armies revolved. And all the Allied commanders listened to the advice of French intelligence.

Now that he had orders to report to the mansion ahead of him, Indiana Jones had reached the big leagues of spying. He could hardly wait to meet his control officer. The plans hatched by French intelligence had an effect on the whole war.

Stopping at the mansion's gate, Indy slipped out his official papers. As Indy watched the guard read them, he saw rainwater dripping from the soldier's shaggy *poilu* mustache.

"I should grow a mustache," Indy thought for about the hundredth time. "Maybe it would make me look older." That could be a helpful thing for an army captain who hadn't seen his eighteenth birthday yet. Then Indy remembered the last time he'd tried—and the sparse collection of hairs that had sprouted on his upper lip.

His thoughts were interrupted as a snappy

Delahaye roadster pulled up in the gateway. Indy took one glance over his shoulder at the khaki-clad pair in the car—British officers, he figured.

He swiveled his head forward again, pretending to ignore the "Out of the way!" honk the driver gave him.

"Your papers, Captain Défense," the guard said. Indy took the papers and began pedaling down the long driveway. "Défense" was the name he'd chosen when he'd signed up. At least it sounded more Belgian than "Jones." He'd risen quickly; in less than a year, he'd gone from messenger to special agent.

Indy was only halfway to the mansion when he heard the auto roaring up on him. Sure, he realized, the guard wouldn't bother asking for papers from officers driving a fancy car.

The two-tone roadster came barreling up the drive, nearly forcing Indy off.

"Oaf!" Indy heard the driver mutter.

It was a struggle to keep the bike upright and on the road. Wet branches from the shrubs at the side smacked into Indy's slicker as he swerved. But that was the least he had to worry about.

The passage of hundreds of cars had worn

away the gravel cover on the driveway. And rain had mixed with the revealed dirt to create a large mud puddle. The wheels of the onrushing car caught the puddle right in the middle, sending a huge spray of water gushing in Indy's direction.

He braked, closing his eyes as chilly water deluged him. Not only did he get soaked through, he could feel a trickle of mud snaking under his uniform collar. It seemed that no matter where he went in this war, the muck and mire were waiting for him.

When Indy opened his eyes, the Delahaye was parked in the courtyard of the mansion. The two khaki-clad figures were already up the stone steps of the building, being greeted at the door.

Indy gritted his teeth, glaring after the pair of men, who entered as if they were royalty. He'd seen enough upper-class British arrogance from his school days. Wartime didn't seem to make the officers any more polite to what they considered "lower classes."

"With allies like those," Indy muttered, "who needs enemies?"

Chapter 2

Colonel Belmond of military intelligence stood with his back to the arched window of his office, ignoring the gray day outside.

At the doorway, the colonel's aide, Major Delon, ushered two young khaki-clad officers into the office. "Right this way, Lieutenants," the major said.

To Belmond's eyes, the young men looked a bit out of place in uniform. With their handsome faces and carefully slicked dark hair, they should have been in a fashion magazine. Perhaps as models wearing polo outfits, evening clothes, or smoking jackets. And drinking champagne.

The older lieutenant drew off tight leather driving gloves, tossed them in his uniform cap, and looked eagerly at the colonel.

"Gentlemen," Belmond said, "President Poincaré and Prime Minister Briand have given your proposal due consideration."

"And?" The lieutenant nervously twisted his gloves and cap in his hand.

"They feel your plan is a risk," Belmond admitted. Then he gave them a sly smile. "But a daring and brilliant risk. They've given their complete approval."

The two young officers whooped in triumph, slapping each other on the back. Belmond stepped forward to shake their hands. "I'd say a toast was in order. Major, would you be so kind?"

"With pleasure, sir." Major Delon was already at the liquor cabinet. "Cognac?"

The older lieutenant took his glass. "This is extraordinary news. Colonel, if you would, be sure to thank the president and prime minister for us." He spoke as if he were used to hobnobbing with the highest in the land.

10

Belmond raised his glass. "Gentlemen, God speed you in your efforts."

"Here, here!" Delon said.

The men drank soldier-style, knocking back their brandy. Slamming his glass down, the older lieutenant, still the spokesman, turned to the colonel. "When do we leave?"

"Immediately," Belmond told him. "You'll be supplied with false papers, disguises . . ."

The younger officer, a little finer-boned than his older brother, broke in excitedly. "False papers! Disguises!"

Smiling at the young man's enthusiasm, Belmond went on. "And, of course, an agent."

"An agent?" the older brother repeated, leaning forward. His eyes showed the same excitement as he whispered, "A *spy*?"

"Precisely that," Belmond said, turning to Delon. "Major, show in Captain Défense."

Grinning broadly, the two brothers tried to control their enthusiasm. But the younger man couldn't help himself. "Imagine, Sixtus," he burst out, "our very own spy. Wait till the ladies at the club hear about this."

Sixtus chuckled. "Xavier, I'll bet he's a right ruffian. Great coarse fellow with knives in his boots and a scar across his throat—"

11

"Probably missing an ear!" Xavier added. "I can't wait to meet him."

The laughter came to an abrupt end when Delon led in Indiana Jones, still dripping muddy water.

"This can't be our spy," Sixtus stammered. "Surely there's a mistake."

"No mistake," Belmond assured him.

"A spy? Really?" Xavier said. "But he's so young."

"We passed him on the way in." Sixtus glanced from the driving gloves in his hand to Indy's muddy boots. "We thought he was an errand boy."

Indy pulled a khaki cap from under his slicker, flicking its small golden tassel with his finger. He also opened his slicker, revealing two small gold stars on his tunic. Close up, he realized these officers wore Belgian uniforms, as he did, not British kit.

Indy looked pointedly at the single silver stars on their tunic collars. "That's '*Captain* Errand Boy' to you, Second Lieutenant," he said. "And unless you're dressed for a masquerade, I fully expect to be saluted."

"Captain, really!" Belmond huffed, with an anxious glance at his aristocratic guests.

"No, no, he's quite right." Sixtus snapped off a salute, then glanced at his brother Xavier, who still stood, staring. The younger man needed a nudge before he finally saluted. Indy responded with a crisp salute of his own.

"Our apologies, Captain," Sixtus said.

Belmond frowned as he watched this performance. "You clearly have no idea who these gentlemen are," he finally said.

"Two officers of junior rank?" Indy suggested. To his eyes, they looked like a pair of rich young idiots who'd decided that snappy uniforms might impress the girls in nightclubs.

Belmond's frown deepened. "These are the brothers Prince Sixtus and Prince Xavier of Bourbon-Parma."

"Charmed, I'm sure," Indy said flippantly.

Belmond glanced at his royal visitors. "They are, in fact, the reason you've been summoned here. You are assigned to a very delicate task."

"You see," Prince Xavier spoke up, "our sister is the Empress Zita of Austria . . ."

Indy's eyebrows rose. "That's awkward, considering we're at war with Austria."

"You all know the war situation," Belmond said, pointing to the map over his desk. "Our enemies, the Central Powers—Germany,

13

Austria-Hungary, Bulgaria, and Turkey—stretch across the middle of Europe. They are faced on the west and south by France, Britain, Belgium, and Italy. To the east, cut off from us, is Russia."

He swept a hand around the enemy nations. "As things stand, the German kaiser and his allies can quickly shift troops around their central position, blocking any of our attacks." Now Belmond's hand slapped against Austria-Hungary. "But Austria is the keystone, the link between Germany in the north and her allies to the south and east."

"Our sister recently had a letter smuggled to us," Xavier explained eagerly. "She begs us to come to Vienna with all haste. It seems her husband, Emperor Karl, wishes to negotiate a peace settlement separate from Germany."

Indy slowly stared from the young prince to the map. "That would pull the rug right out from underneath the kaiser, force his hand in ending this war."

Xavier nodded. "Germany would have to concede. They'd have no choice."

Indy turned to Belmond. "What would my part be in this?"

"You are to escort Lieutenants Sixtus and

Xavier into Vienna," Belmond said. "There, they will meet secretly with Emperor Karl and try to secure in writing certain concessions demanded by our government. Then you will get the brothers safely back to France . . . with the letter."

Prince Sixtus leaned forward. "If we succeed, we can end this war with the stroke of a pen . . . without another shot fired or another life lost. Are you interested?"

Indy's eyes went back to the map—to the ribbon of death known as the Western Front. A slow smile came to his face as he nodded.

The Gare de Lyon was huge and cavernous, one of the major Parisian railway stations. And, as Indy discovered, wartime kept the platforms crowded. Porters carried luggage for young officers on their way to the front. Steam engines billowed smoke. The sounds of hissing engines, ringing bells, and thousands of conversations echoed off the vaulted roof.

At last, Indy spotted Colonel Belmond and Major Delon. But when he saw Sixtus and Xavier, his heart sank. As planned, all three members of the secret mission wore civilian clothes. Indy had a heavy tweed belted jacket, stout wool pants, hiking boots, and, of course, his good-luck fedora hat.

Xavier stood with a velvet-collared gray overcoat thrown over his shoulders. His black suit was perfectly tailored, as was his gray double-breasted vest. With a homburg hat and a slightly too floppy bow tie, he made a dashing fashion statement.

Sixtus, on the other hand, wore what he probably considered a rough-and-ready checked suit, with a tan cashmere polo coat and a soft hat. Both men had delicately pointed handmade shoes that wouldn't last two miles if they had to hike in the country.

Indy shook his head. So this was princes' idea of dressing inconspicuously. Xavier looked as if he owned half the banks in Vienna.

As for Sixtus—well, he'd tried. But the cravat under his high collar was worth a month's wages for an ordinary worker. And the gold stickpin had cost enough for that worker to live on for a year.

Belmond spoke. "These are your papers," he said, and Indy turned to receive a packet from the colonel. "They're expert forgeries and should see you safely into Austria."

Delon nodded. "Once across the border, you will be contacted by our operative, with further instructions."

"Operative?" Indy asked, tucking the papers into an inside pocket.

"Schultz," the colonel said.

Indy sighed. It wasn't enough, setting off on a dangerous mission with two absolute amateurs. His superior had to start playing twenty questions. "How will I find this . . . 'Schultz'?"

Major Delon leaned close, his whisper almost a hiss. "Schultz will find *you*."

Behind them, the whistle on their train sounded. Indy shepherded the two princes aboard. Their faces still shone with the excitement of their great adventure.

Indiana Jones wanted to shake the silliness out of them. Then he remembered the way he had felt—and probably looked—when he first went off to war.

Oh well, Indy thought. They'll learn otherwise soon enough.

Chapter 3

As the train chugged through rolling French countryside beginning to bloom with spring greenery, the horrors of war seemed a thousand miles away. Certainly, Indiana Jones noted with annoyance, Sixtus and Xavier seemed to think so.

Indy tried to sleep—he'd learned the soldier's trick of napping whenever he could. But it wasn't easy. The princes filled the train compartment with chatter about nightclubs and society balls.

He gave up any pretense of sleeping as they reached the foothills of the Alps. Xavier treated him to a discussion on the skiing at Gstaad. Then came a long story, some scandal about people he'd never heard of—the Duke and Duchess of Somewhere or Other.

Indy couldn't stand it anymore. Putting his fingers to his lips, he let out a shrill, deafening whistle.

"Let's get one thing straight," he said as the royal brothers stared at him, openmouthed. "We're not here on holiday. This is a damn serious business."

A flush rose on Sixtus's face. "I don't think we need you to tell us that."

"I think you do," Indy told him bluntly. "Look at you—you're dressed like a couple of Parisian dandies off to the gaming tables."

The brothers glanced at each other, as if they'd just noticed what they were wearing. Then Xavier said quietly, "You don't like us much, do you?"

"I don't care for the frivolous. In this kind of work it can get you killed." Indy gave them a hard look. How could he explain the harsh truths of intelligence work to these overgrown Boy Scouts? "If we go into Austria with you prattling on about Gstaad this and the Duke and Duchess of that, they'll be on to us in no time."

"Who?" Sixtus demanded. "German spies?"

"The German spies don't concern me so much," Indy said. "All they'd do is shoot us."

"Shoot us? Really?" Prince Xavier's handsome face went pale.

Indy smiled at him fiendishly. "I'm more worried about the Austrian secret police."

Sixtus looked puzzled. "What would they do?"

"Poke our eyes out, strip our flesh, feed us our innards . . ." Indy said airily. "For starters."

He ended his recitation when he saw the queasy looks on the princes' faces. "Look, the government has turned control of Austria over to the military. There are no rights, no trials—just military court-martials. They don't mind using terror to get what they want. And if they want information from us . . ." Indy left that thought dangling.

"But—but surely there are the rules of war," Prince Sixtus protested.

"Oh, they signed a piece of paper in Holland some years back," Indy agreed, half smiling. "But that provides no protection for soldiers caught behind the lines out of uniform. You're a spy now, Prince. Expecting to be treated like an officer and a gentleman—that's frivolous."

"You may view us as frivolous, Captain," Xavier said haughtily. "But let me assure you, my brother was very active in public affairs back in Paris. Which wasn't easy, considering the laws against members of our family."

"They have laws against your family?" Indy held back a laugh. "What are you? Public enemies?"

"To some people we are," Sixtus admitted. "We're Bourbons, descended from the old French royal family. France is a democracy now, and many Frenchmen want to keep it that way."

"So you may view us as frivolous," Xavier said, "but our commitment to ending this horror is not."

"Oh, poor little rich boys. No one takes them seriously." Indy glared at the princes. "Look, you two. I've *seen* the horror you're talking about. Flanders, Verdun, the Congo." He blinked his eyes, trying to push away the images of too many dead bodies. "How much horror have you glimpsed from the Paris nightclubs?"

"Those uniforms we wear aren't just for

show," Sixtus said. "My brother and I serve as stretcher-bearers, carrying the wounded off the front lines."

Xavier shuddered. "We've seen how living men are ground up like sausages by the artillery shells and machine guns. Our sister is equally concerned." He suddenly turned to his brother. "Sixtus, show him the letter."

Reaching into an inner pocket of his suit jacket, Sixtus brought out a folded piece of paper. Indy began reading the letter aloud.

" 'Do not think of yourselves. Think of all those unfortunate souls living in the hell of the trenches, dying there every day by the thousands, and come with all haste.' "

Indy thought of his friend Rémy Baudouin, still on the firing line, trapped in the hell the empress wrote about. A smile came to his lips as he put a hand in one pocket. "I like your sister already."

His hand came out of the pocket holding a match, which he flicked with his thumbnail. As the match blazed up, he touched its flame to the empress's letter.

Sixtus bounded from his seat, snatching furiously for the burning sheet of paper. "You pig!" he shouted. "How dare you?"

Indy set down the shriveling letter. "Just how far do you think we'll get if they search you at the border and find this?"

Sixtus clicked his mouth shut and dropped back into his seat.

"We hadn't thought of that," Xavier said in a small voice.

"No. You hadn't," Indy agreed sarcastically. By now, the paper had been reduced to ashes. He scooped them up and tossed them out the open window. "But you'd better start thinking like that if you want to come through this little adventure in one piece."

Chapter 4

An hour after their train crossed the Swiss border, Indy dug a length of string out of his pocket. He tied it into a loop, spread it between his hands, and began playing cat's cradle. As he worked the string into more and more complex patterns between his fingers, the royal brothers talked about their war work.

"We tried to join the French army," Xavier explained. "Sixtus says that a Bourbon is always French. But we were prevented by law because of our Bourbon heritage."

"So you joined the Belgian army instead."
Indy thought about how he'd sneaked into that
country's service under a false name. The three
of them would make a great recruiting poster:
WE'LL TAKE ANYBODY. He grinned. "No law
prevented you from signing on with them?" he
asked.

"Well . . . Cousin Albert did pull a few
strings," Xavier admitted.

"Cousin Albert?" Indy asked.

"The king of Belgium," Sixtus explained.

Indy looked up from the pattern he was con-
structing. "Cousin Albert is the king of
Belgium?"

The brothers nodded as Indy went on. "And
Sister Zita is the empress of Austria . . ."

"She married Karl a few years before the war
broke out. He was only an archduke then,"
Sixtus said. "I've followed reports on his military service. He's a stalwart chap, even though
he's the enemy."

As he listened to this story, Indy continued
weaving his cat's cradle. But the strings became more and more tangled. "Is there a
Crowned Head of Europe you're not related to?"
he finally burst out.

Xavier pursed his lips. "I'd have to think about

that. I imagine we're all bound in some way or other, by blood or marriage."

Indy rolled his eyes. "Next you'll be telling me you're related to the kaiser."

Xavier looked questioningly at Sixtus, who shrugged. "I'm not sure," Sixtus finally said. "We might have a connection with Czar Nicholas on Great-Grandmama's side . . ."

The strings were nearly strangling Indy's fingers as he looked up. "What does the czar of Russia have to do with this?"

"He and the kaiser are cousins," Xavier said helpfully. "So is King George of England."

Looking down at the tangled mess on his hands, Indy tore the cat's cradle loose and threw the string away. "The entire world is at war because your family can't get along," he complained, shaking his head. "I'm going to sleep. Gentlemen, I suggest you do the same. After all, we don't know what's waiting for us in Austria."

The conductor woke them as the train pulled to a stop at the border checkpoint. Indy, Sixtus, and Xavier opened the outer compartment door, stumbling off into darkness.

A soldier stepped into the light spilling from the door, and Indy almost jumped. The man's uniform was field gray, the same color the

Germans wore. Then Indy noticed the old-fashioned military cap on the soldier's head. Of course—this was a Swiss militiaman. Switzerland had called up almost all its able-bodied men to protect its neutrality.

"This way," the soldier directed.

As they came up to a crowd of passengers, Indy whispered, "Remember, we don't know one another," to the two princes. Separating, they blended in with the shuffling group of travelers.

The emptied train huffed gently across the border. Indy watched as a well-trained squad of Austrian troopers climbed aboard to search the cars.

On either side of the tracks, a high fence marked the dividing line between countries. It would have been hard enough to climb even without the tangles of barbed wire stretched across the top. The glare of massed search-lights blinded Indy as they shone over the fence, lighting up the train, sometimes tracing a way over the crowd.

Anyone trying to leave Austria would not only face a stiff climb, but would have to dodge those lights—and the bullets that would surely follow.

The line of passengers moved slowly forward as Austrian border guards began examining papers. Xavier was through already, Indy saw as he handed his papers to a red-faced Austrian sergeant. After being waved through, Indy winked at the younger prince. He didn't let the fear show in his eyes until he turned to glance back at the crossing.

Sixtus was standing with the sergeant now. "Are these your papers, *mein Herr*?" the soldier asked.

"Of course they're my papers." Sixtus spoke like a man who'd handled difficult headwaiters for years. "I assure you they're in order. Now if you would let me pass . . ."

Instead, the sergeant turned to a tall, thin figure in a long black trench coat. Indy couldn't see the man's face under the wide brim of a black slouch hat. But he knew the type. This had to be an officer of the Austrian secret police.

As the figure stepped forward, similar black-clad figures seemed to appear from nowhere. "Here now—!" Sixtus began. But he was quickly hustled off by secret-police agents and soldiers.

The search squad suddenly poured off the train. The last soldier off turned to the passengers. "All clear!" he called. "You may re-board!"

Passengers hurried toward their carriages, but Indy lagged behind. Just as well: He was able to grab onto Xavier's arm before the young prince could run back to the crossing gate.

"They're taking him away!" Xavier whispered, agony in his eyes. "We have to *do* something!"

Chapter 5

Somehow, Indy manhandled Xavier aboard the train and into their compartment. The young man collapsed on a seat as the train lurched forward. "My poor, poor brother. Whatever shall I tell our sister? Whatever shall I tell our *mother*?"

Indy didn't know what to say. There was nothing they could do. Xavier would only have gotten them killed as well. Then who would complete their mission?

"You could tell them the silly fools at the

border mistook me for someone else," a voice boomed from the passageway door. Sixtus grinned at them.

"Sixtus! We thought you were a goner!" Xavier leaped up to embrace his brother.

"So did I!" Sixtus admitted. "I was searched." He glanced at Indy. "Thank God you burned that letter."

Indy, however, didn't feel relieved. He sat back down, frowning.

Sixtus gave him a worried look. "What are you thinking?"

"Why arrest us at the border?" Indy said slowly. "Why not shadow us into Vienna and smash the entire spy network?"

The brothers stood in silence for a long moment, letting that thought sink in.

"But surely we'd have noticed by now if someone were following us." Indy noticed that in spite of the protest, Sixtus kept his voice down.

And a good thing he had, Indy thought as the passageway door to the compartment slid open with a loud rasp.

A short, fat woman stood in the doorway. She wore a traveling outfit about twenty years out of date. A pair of bulging blue eyes stared at

31

them over bulging, doughy cheeks. Where her traveling cloak opened, a pair of black, shoe-button eyes glared at them. The eyes belonged to the tiny dachshund the woman held under her coat.

Great, Indy thought. That little beast looks more like an overfed rat.

"Guten abend," the woman said.

The three men responded with stiff nods. "Good evening," Xavier replied, also in German.

"This seat is taken?" she asked, pointing to the empty space beside Indy. As she sat down, the little wiener dog snapped at Indy's elbow. "Quiet, Schatze."

Silence curdled in the small train compartment. Indy and the others couldn't discuss their mission in front of a stranger—especially one who might be a secret-police spy.

At last, Sixtus and Xavier nodded off. Indy sat for a while, sneaking sidelong glances at his seatmate. How could a face that pudgy look so stern? Finally, ignoring Schatze's beady, hostile eyes, Indy fell into a doze.

He woke to an annoying clicking sound. Across the compartment, Xavier and Sixtus tossed fitfully in their seats, at least half asleep.

But the other passenger sat fully awake, her pop eyes taking everything in. As for the clicking, that was the woman's knitting needles, busily working away at some unidentifiable garment.

Row after row of stitches rolled off those blasted needles with nerve-racking precision. Was that a woman over there, Indy wondered, or a knitting machine? Most annoying, by the time the train reached Amstetten, their destination, he still hadn't been able to figure out what the woman was knitting.

Sixtus and Xavier stood on the station platform, looking like a pair of stranded tourists. Indy had his hands in his pockets; he was quietly scanning the station entrance.

"Now what?" Sixtus asked.

"We make contact with Schultz. Or rather, he makes contact with us." Indy continued his covert observation. "I wonder what this Schultz looks like?"

A low snarl came from behind them. Indy, Xavier, and Sixtus whirled to be confronted by two sets of eyes—one pair blue and bulging, the others beady little doggie ones.

The woman from the train shook her head in disgust. "I am Schultz," she said. "Come." Indy and the princes sheepishly followed.

Schultz had a pretty little country cottage, complete with a tiled fireplace. The moment she was in the door, she set a blaze. Then she collected the men's forged papers and threw them in. "Change in the other room."

Moments later, she brought in new papers. "The three gentlemen who entered Austria by train no longer exist. Now there are only three young Austrian soldiers on leave."

Xavier had already finished putting on his field-gray uniform. Now he picked up his officer's peaked cap, setting it on his head at a rakish angle. "I always thought we should be captains."

Sixtus flicked the three stars on his tunic collar. "Now, *Lieutenant* . . . unless you're dressed for a masquerade, we fully expect to be saluted."

Indy, still buttoning up his tunic (which had only *one* star), gritted his teeth. "Don't press your royal luck," he warned.

The brothers chuckled as Schultz gave them their new identity papers. When she came to Indy, however, Schultz gave him car keys and a note as well. "Take the car in the shed outside and go to Vienna," she said. "Go to this address. Tell them you are friends of Frederick. He'll take you from there."

The car turned out to be an ancient Benz. But it started after a few cranks, and Indy and the princes enjoyed a bracing open-air journey down the Danube River. Greenery was just appearing in the fields, and on the branches of the trees in the woods.

They passed over a high-arched stone bridge, so old that Indy could imagine knights in armor using it. The country became hillier, with vineyards cropping up. Then they were driving through woodland so heavy that the road seemed like a tunnel, roofed by branches.

Reaching the crest of a hill, they suddenly saw the land before them spread out in a huge plain. And as far as his eyes could take in, Indy saw Vienna. There was the grayish bulk of St. Stephen's Cathedral, with *der Steffl*, its enormous steeple. Brownish government office buildings stood next to white marble palaces. And all over were the red tile rooftops of the everyday city-dwellers.

For a moment, Indy smiled down at the vista, remembering happier times. Nine years ago, his father had taken him to the Austrian capital.

That visit had brought him adventure, a command of the German language, and a special friend: little Sophie, who was going to grow up to become an archduchess.

The smile faded from Indy's lips. Sophie *was* grown up now. And her father, the Archduke Franz Ferdinand, had been the first to die in this crazy war, brought down by an assassin's bullet.

Indy abruptly shoved the car into gear. "The address Schultz gave us is in the old city," he said. "We can head straight down from up here."

Soon enough, they were driving along a wide *Strasse.* The street was lined with the overdecorated buildings of the Baroque era. Sixtus and Xavier were having a fine old time, sitting in the backseat of the Benz. They tipped their peaked caps to young women on the sidewalks. Xavier kept trying to fit a monocle under his right eyebrow.

As Indy turned off the wider street, the buildings became less palatial, more homelike. And the girls were dressed less expensively. The smaller the streets, Indy noticed, the more crooked and old-fashioned they became. He began to wish that Schultz had given him a map instead of an address.

At last Indy took the car around a corner and hit the brakes. The street beyond was extremely modest, the kind where people lived in garrets up four or five flights of stairs. So why was it blocked off?

As he looked over the crowd, he picked out uniforms—police and military field-gray—moving among the civilians. Xavier peered at a street sign attached to a peeling whitewashed wall. "Say, isn't that where we're supposed to go?"

Sixtus rose up in the backseat. "I can see the address from here."

The door with the address number on it swung open to reveal a man in uniform. He carried a stretcher with a still, sheet-covered form on it. That was the beginning of a regular procession. Before Indy could count how many dead bodies were coming out, a policeman stepped up, waving them on. "What happened?" Indy asked.

"A terrible shoot-out," the young officer told him excitedly. "Terrible." He leaned forward, lowering his voice. "I'm told the secret police broke up a ring of spies."

The crowd opened, and a black-clad figure stepped out. For secret police, these guys seem to have a pretty high profile, Indy thought.

Straightening up, the policeman suddenly began gesturing fiercely. Obviously, he'd also noticed the approach of the agent. "Turn your car around and go back the way you came! Move along!"

Sixtus gave him a nervous glance. "Lieutenant," he said to Indy, "I suggest you do as the policeman says."

Indy quickly threw the gearshift into reverse. As the car rolled back, he spotted another figure in black, moving against the flow of curious onlookers. This man's trench coat was a little shabby, his fedora hat battered on his shaven head. Was this a low-ranking secret policeman?

Please let us get to a wider street so I can turn and get out of here, Indy prayed. Just as he got the car turned around, the shabby black-clad man appeared beside them. "Stop the car!" he hissed.

Instead, Indy tromped on the gas. But the man surprised him with a burst of speed, leaping onto the running board of the car and tearing open the door. A second later he was in the car.

Now Indy hit the brakes, sending the car into a skid. Everyone aboard was jolted, and heads on the sidewalk began to turn. The man in black glared at him. "First you go, now you stop! Drive, you idiot!"

Indy stared into the man's dark, sunken eyes. "I don't think so."

"You are friends of Frederick, *ja*?"

"Frederick? Yes, we know Freder—Oof!" Xavier's words were cut off by an elbow in the ribs from Sixtus. "I mean I *knew* a Frederick once, back in school . . ."

"I think you've mistaken us for someone else." Indy's voice was low and deadly.

The intruder's eyes shifted from Indy to the crowd in the street. His gaunt face went tighter as he noticed a policeman staring at them. "I am a friend of Frederick, too. Now *drive*. We're drawing attention."

"We don't know you, friend," Indy insisted. "We're not going anywhere."

The man dropped into the seat beside Indy, leaning toward him. When his hand came out of his raincoat pocket, he was holding a heavy Luger pistol. Giving Indy a skeleton's grin, he hissed, "Trust me."

With a gun in his ribs, Indy had no choice. As the policeman began heading for them, Indy hit the gas again.

Chapter 6

Indy knew that the automatic pistol pressed into his ribs usually held seven bullets. He also knew that one pull on the trigger would send a slug nearly half an inch wide tearing through him at three hundred miles an hour.

That was why he did exactly what the stranger who'd just boarded the car told him to do. The old Benz rolled down the street, heading back toward the larger boulevards. Sixtus and Xavier sat in paralyzed silence in the backseat. They had seen the gun in the man's hand.

Luckily, the police hadn't. They turned away from the Benz as the old automobile stopped blocking the road.

"Who are you?" Indy asked through tight lips. He tried to sound calm, but a drop of sweat crawled down the side of his face.

"You may call me Mr. Max," their gaunt uninvited guest said. He peered down the road they were traveling. "Turn left," he commanded sharply.

"Whatever you say." Indy winced as the Luger jarred with bruising force into his side. "But we still don't know any Frederick."

That got him another death's-head grin from Mr. Max. "No?" he asked. "Then why were you going to that house? Three nice Austrian soldier boys like you. Nothing better to do on your furlough than visit a nest of spies?"

Indy gave no answer, but more droplets of sweat appeared on his face.

The gaunt man's sharp, sunken eyes scanned behind them for anyone tailing. "Turn right," he snapped.

For the next hour or so, Mr. Max took them on a zigzagging tour of the poorer neighborhoods ringing Vienna's central city. He even ordered them across one of the steel suspension bridges spanning the Danube River, then back over again.

At last, they wound up in one of the industrial suburbs on the heights overlooking the city. Indy was surprised when Mr. Max told him to stop.

Their destination looked like an old farmhouse, although it was in the middle of a built-up area. Blocks of city-type tenements surrounded them.

The old building's rough plaster walls hadn't been whitewashed in years, and factory grime hung heavy on the red tile roof. Indy couldn't read the dingy sign except for one word: KAF-FEESIEDER.

"A coffeehouse?" Judging by the tone of Sixtus's voice, he'd been expecting a large gray building with SECRET POLICE carved over the door.

"I thought you would like something to drink while I arrange for the next step on your journey." The gaunt man gave them another of those disconcerting smiles as he led them out of the car.

The inside of the café was as dark and murky as the outside was grimy. Tobacco smoke hung in the air, and Indy was surprised to see how crowded the place was. A fat man in a greasy black suit gave them an oily greeting.

"Herr Otto," Mr. Max said with his skull-like smile, "a dark one for each of my friends."

"Of course, Herr Doktor Max. Come, gentlemen, sit." Herr Otto led them to a table by the window, while Mr. Max went to the café's phone. A moment later, four tiny cups of coffee had appeared. Indy ignored his, leaning out to try and catch what their captor/guide was saying.

"Yes, I have them. How soon can you be here?" Mr. Max saw Indy and turned his back.

"I don't trust this 'Mr. Max,' " Sixtus said, staring suspiciously at the man's worn trench coat.

"He seems to know all about us," Xavier pointed out in a hopeful whisper. "He could be working with Frederick."

Indy frowned, taking in the people around them, trying to figure the angles and come up with a plan. "He could also be from the secret police. They could have beaten that information out of Frederick when they arrested him."

Sixtus's look went from suspicious to worried. "So what do we do?"

"Play along—for now." Indy absently sipped

43

his coffee, staring out the dingy window. The café was on one of the last hills overlooking Vienna. The whole city was spread out below him in the gathering dusk. Beyond the spires and roofs, lights were coming on in the Prater, Vienna's playground. Years ago, Indy had visited the carnivals out there. It was like a fairyland for a young boy.

Section by section, a large construction sprang into light. Indy smiled with nostalgia. It was the *Riesenrad*, Vienna's huge Ferris wheel. When he'd last visited the city, it had seemed like a symbol of Vienna—bright, gaudy, larger than life. The whole edge of the wheel glowed now, and the spokes of the wheel lit up.

Unfortunately, Indy was quickly reminded of what Vienna meant in 1917 when a skull-like face pushed into his view, giving him a devil's smile. "We Viennese are proud of our Ferris wheel," Mr. Max said. "Espresso to your liking?"

Indy jerked back, lifting his cup and finishing it without tasting. "It's fine."

"Fine?" Xavier broke in, staring at his cup in disgust. "This so-called coffee tastes like boiled tree bark."

"Don't let Herr Otto hear," Mr. Max cautioned in a low voice. "He wouldn't want his recipe to get out."

Indy noticed that the gaunt man played with his cup, but didn't drink any coffee. "It is the war," Mr. Max explained in a whisper. "We get less and less food in Vienna. And it becomes more and more expensive. Unless this ends, people will starve."

Yes, Indy realized, Vienna had changed very much since his last visit. "So now what?" he asked.

"Now we wait." Mr. Max pushed his cup away. "Frederick is dead, in case you're wondering."

"Sorry to hear that." Privately, Indy wondered if he, Sixtus, and Xavier would wind up the same way.

The skull face in front of him suddenly looked tired. "These are sad times in Austria," Mr. Max muttered. "Ours is an empire of many nationalities. Internal strife is tearing the country apart. For too many of our leaders, it's much more expedient—simpler—just to kill people nowadays."

Two men in trench coats came through the

café door, heading straight for their table. Mr. Max abruptly stood. "These men will see to you. I do hope it's over quickly."

With an ironic little bow, the strange man left them to their fate. Indy stared poker-faced as the new arrivals came at them. He and the princes were sitting ducks, trapped at the table.

The first trench-coated figure had a tight face marked with acne. He counted out money to pay for the coffee. Indy couldn't believe how expensive it was. At least Herr Otto was happy with the tip. The other newcomer stood back— covering them, Indy realized.

"Come," the first stranger said curtly.

Farther back in the café, two figures sat at the bar. One looked as if he'd just stepped out of an anti-German propaganda poster. His hair was cut so short that his bullet-shaped head seemed shaven. A roll of fat from his thick neck pushed over his collar. His monocle flashed in the dim light.

The other man was huge, bulky, and over-muscled—the kind of fighter who takes a lot of killing. He was missing an ear, and a necklace of dead-white scar tissue twisted across his throat.

The monocled German gestured after Mr. Max. "Follow him, Mabuse."

"*Jawohl,* Count von Büler." The big man tossed back his glass of schnapps and left.

Von Büler tossed a few coins on the bar, got up, and started after the other group—the one including young Indiana Jones.

Chapter 7

Young Indiana Jones shifted on the cracked leather seat of what had once been an expensive limousine. He was *not* a happy spy.

The men in trench coats who had invaded the café had led them to this car and hustled them aboard. Settled in the back, Indy noticed that his window had been painted over. So was the rear windshield.

Sixtus peered through the glass panel that separated the chauffeur from the backseats. "We missed the turn," he said, his voice going high.

"Schönbrunn Palace is back that way. This isn't the route to the emperor's palace."

Indy tapped on the panel until the second man, thin and pale-faced, turned. "Hey! We're going the wrong way!"

The pale face turned away without a word. Indy grabbed for the door handle. It didn't budge.

They drove on for what seemed to be forever, leaving the lights of the city behind. Great, Indy told himself. They aren't even going to bother questioning us. They're just taking us to a nice quiet spot for execution.

At last, the car drew up in front of a massive iron gate in a huge stone wall. A double flash of the headlights, and the gates opened to reveal a dark, flagstoned courtyard.

"As soon as they open the doors," Indy whispered, "we jump them. Agreed?"

Sixtus nodded. "Devil take the consequences."

The trench-coated men unlocked the door, and Indy and his friends leaped out, ready to attack.

But the three prisoners staggered to a halt when they saw they weren't alone. A dozen cloaked figures in shining silver helmets with white plumes stood around them, leveling rifles.

Indy forced his eyes away from the gun muzzles to see where they were. Behind the limo was a spiked iron gate, and all around he saw tall stone walls. The open space seemed too small to be a prison yard, and he decided the soldiers were too well dressed to be a firing squad. Maybe they were in the forecourt of a castle.

He decided to go quietly as the trench-coated men led the way to a low, iron-banded wooden door set into one of the walls. Besides, with all the guards around, there wasn't much he or the princes could do.

Indy found himself shivering as they marched down a dank, dripping passageway. The slimy stone seemed to draw any warmth away.

Dozens of footsteps echoed off the walls and ceiling. Was it Indy's imagination, or did the passage seem to lead downward?

Their silent escort came to a halt before a pair of massive wooden doors set into ancient stone walls. The men in trench coats stepped forward, grasping the heavy iron rings bolted to the wood.

Beside him, Indy heard Sixtus and Xavier take

deep breaths. What would they find beyond there? A torture chamber? Executioners?

The doors swung open with surprising quietness. Indy and the princes stood gaping. For a second they were blinded by the light gleaming from gold candelabra and a crystal chandelier. The stone floor was hidden under a huge, thick Oriental rug. Beautifully woven tapestries covered the walls of the room.

A long table, covered with snowy white linen, gleaming china, and shining silverware, dominated the room. Only two people were seated there: a regal-looking young woman with dark hair, and a uniformed young man with a dark mustache and an open, handsome face.

The young man threw down his napkin as he leaped to his feet, beaming. "Sixtus! Xavier!" he cried. "Finally! We'd just about given up on you!"

Sixtus stepped into the room. "So had we, Karl, so had we!"

Rising from the table, Empress Zita rushed to her brothers, her white gown fluttering. She flung her arms around Sixtus and Xavier, pulling them in. Emperor Karl gave the princes a couple of hearty backslaps. Indy stepped into the room, feeling out of place at the big family

51

reunion. Behind him, the wooden doors closed with a muffled *boom*.

Karl turned to Indy. "And who is this third man?"

Sixtus took on the introductions.

"Captain Henri Défense—our spy!"

"He got us into Vienna," Xavier explained. "If not for him, Lord knows what would have become of us."

Zita stepped up, every inch an empress. "Well done, Captain. We are most grateful."

Karl turned to the two trench-coated agents, who now stood by the closed doors. "Summon Count Czernin immediately," he ordered. "Tell him the package has arrived."

Count Ottokar Czernin was a tall, thin, distinguished man, who kept his dignity whether being introduced to princes or to spies. He sat in a heavy chair in a drawing room, frowning in thought as he listened.

Karl leaned against the mantelpiece of the huge marble fireplace, where a cheery blaze roared. Zita and her brothers sat on beautifully carved, spindly furniture. Indy stood off to one side. He wondered how the count, a trained diplomatic professional, was taking the princes' message. He couldn't tell from any facial expressions. Indy figured the count would make a dandy poker player.

Sixtus, on the other hand, looked very serious as he spoke. The count made notes.

"The French and British governments are most anxious to declare peace with Austria," he said, "but only if Karl is willing to grant three key concessions. In writing."

Count Czernin nodded, his pen ready. "And those are?"

"Number one," Sixtus said. "Austria must renounce all German claims to the region of Alsace-Lorraine . . ."

As Czernin wrote, he muttered, "That would undo the last war France fought with Germany—and lost." He looked up. "Go on."

Sixtus continued. "Two. Austria must recognize Belgian sovereignty and agree to the evacuation of all German troops from Belgian territory . . ."

"Mmm-hmm." Czernin's pen skittered along.

That's the reason I'm fighting this war, Indy thought, risking my life. And all this character says is "Mmm-hmm."

Now Karl spoke up. "Three. We must recognize the Serbian nation's sovereignty and grant a Polish homeland within our borders."

"Serbia, eh?" The count looked up from his note-taking. "We are to deny our victory over Serbia, the country that started this war in the first place? It was Serbia that sent agents across our shared border to stir up rebellion in the southern provinces. Need I remind you that some of those agents murdered your uncle, the Archduke Franz Ferdinand?"

Count Czernin was silent for a moment, then spoke on. "Yet not only must we give up our conquest of this troublemaker state, we must lose additional land, and give it to one of our subject races."

Karl's face went red. "I know who killed my uncle—extremists trying to break our rule over the southern Slavs. And let me tell you, Count, I have served on the Russian Front and fought the Italians. This war has killed many more people than Franz Ferdinand. I would sacrifice much to bring the slaughter to an end."

Czernin looked down. "Your Highness, you know it's not my aim to anger you. I was a faithful servant of your great-uncle Franz Josef—a faithful advisor to your uncle Franz

Ferdinand. . . . But we're not just talking here of peace with France. We're talking of an end to our alliance with Germany." The count looked up sharply. "And that is not a thing to be taken lightly. The kaiser can be a powerful enemy . . ."

He turned to Sixtus and Xavier. "As France and England have already learned."

"I understand that, Count," Karl said. "But that must be weighed against the realities of this war. Obviously we could continue until one side crushes the other completely. . . . But at what cost?"

"It is the *failure* of diplomacy that's gotten us into this mess," Zita burst out.

Czernin looked at her for a moment in shocked silence. It was the look of an old-fashioned gentleman who didn't believe that females should have opinions in politics. Finally, the count spoke. "Your Highness has strong views."

"But she's right, isn't she?" Karl cried out. "Look at Russia! My God, a revolution! The czar deposed by his own subjects! And why? Because they are weary of war."

He glared at his minister. "If we wish to avoid the same thing in Austria, the monarchy must be liberalized and we must give the people what they want: peace, whatever the cost."

"Your Highness—" Czernin began.

"It's not just the men in the trenches I'm trying to save. I don't want to go down in history as the *last* emperor of Austria . . . the one who let a thousand-year monarchy crumble like dust in his fingers."

Count Czernin glanced around the room, from face to earnest face. He looked at the floor. "I'll draft the letter. Will tomorrow be soon enough?"

"As soon as you can, Count. Thank you." Karl turned to his visitors. "You must all be exhausted after your trip—not to mention your adventures."

Indy nodded blearily, suddenly aware of how tired he was.

A servant took him up to a tower bedroom. The room was exactly what he would have expected to find in a palace. But he was too weary to enjoy the rich trappings. All he saw was the bed. He managed to kick off his boots, but the unfamiliar buttons on his uniform tunic were beyond him. He finally fell onto the bed while still in his clothes. One hand went for the pillow, the other for the light.

Outside the walls of Laxenburg Castle, the Austrian emperor's country retreat, a man put down his binoculars. The light in the tower window had just gone out. A satisfied smile crossed the fleshy features of Count von Büler, Germany's spymaster in Vienna.

Well, well, well. The emperor of Austria now had three foreign spies in his palace. Interesting guests. What could they be doing in there? He settled himself for a wait. Soon enough they would come out. And after they were caught, far away from the emperor's protection, he could question them at leisure.

Chapter 8

"It's mine! Let go of it!"

"No! *You* let go!"

Young Indiana Jones stood on the terrace of Laxenburg Castle, watching two little children arguing over a gaily painted wooden horse. Behind him was the family breakfast table, now being cleared by servants.

Before him stretched the gardens of Laxenburg—acres and acres of carefully manicured rolling lawns. Indy wondered how it felt to live in your own private park. But he didn't think it polite to ask the man standing beside him: Emperor Karl.

The emperor shook his head as the little boy, dressed in a sailor suit and short pants, stubbornly held onto the front legs of the horse. His sister, in a white pinafore, clung to the rear legs.

They kept up the tug of war a long moment, until the horse broke apart. The little girl flew backward, landing heavily on the ground. She burst into tears.

The girl's mother, Empress Zita, came sailing up in a long white dress. "Stop this nonsense right now!" she scolded.

The little girl pointed an accusing finger. "He broke it!"

Her older brother held the front part of the horse to his chest. "I did not!" he protested. "*She* broke it!"

Zita was not an empress now, only a mother. "Well, if you made an effort to share your toys instead of fighting over them, *nobody* would have broken it, and you could *both* have played."

She looked sternly at the children. "Instead, each of you winds up with nothing. Am I right?"

The small boy looked sadly down at the broken horse. "Yes, ma'am . . ."

Indy glanced over at the emperor, trying not to grin. "Too bad nations don't have grown-ups to settle their disputes."

Karl sighed. "The problem is that the rulers—kings, emperors, presidents—are *supposed* to be grown-ups. It seemed so much easier in my grandfather's time. A word whispered to a royal cousin at a ball could make an alliance—or end a war."

"Let's hope your royal brother-in-law can do the job," Indy said. "Although he doesn't look very royal right now."

Prince Sixtus of Bourbon-Parma was on his hands and knees, jumping up and down while whinnying like a horse. His noises were almost drowned out by the shrieks of delight from the three-year-old child clinging to his back.

Prince Xavier, on the other hand, looked extra dignified with a tiny toy teacup in his hand. He sat in the grass playing tea party with two little girls.

The scene brought the ghost of a smile to Karl's face. "It's good to have family around again," he said. "It's been far too long."

In the bright morning sunlight, Indy could see the shadows under the emperor's eyes. "You look tired, Your Highness. If you don't mind my saying so."

"I didn't sleep well," Karl admitted. "I *haven't* slept well in the four months since I became emperor."

"It's quite a responsibility," Indy said.

"Not one I expected." Karl strolled along the lawns. "When Zita and I married, we planned for a quiet, uneventful life in the royal court. My uncle, Archduke Ferdinand, was next in line to the throne . . . until that lunatic assassinated him and started this war."

"Enormous consequences for firing a single shot," Indy said.

"It was like pulling the lever that starts an enormous machine," Karl said heavily. "Each nation had the plans all set for the mobilization of its military forces. And none of them wanted to stop and talk, for fear their enemies would mobilize first and crush them."

He shook his head. "Even Kaiser Wilhelm, whom everyone thinks of as the arch-warmonger, tried to call a halt at the last moment. But he couldn't stop the machinery. Now it goes on, grinding up millions of soldiers and civilians."

For a second, Indy debated asking after

Sophie, Franz Ferdinand's daughter. Was she an archduchess now?

He lost his chance when a long black limousine came rolling up to the gates. Sixtus swung the little rider off his back and bounded to his feet. "There's Count Czernin! C'mon, everybody race back to the house!"

He and Xavier led a charge of children back to the palace. Karl smiled sadly as the sounds of childish laughter wafted across the terrace. "I think I would've enjoyed a quiet, uneventful life."

The count was ushered into the drawing room, where the princes, the emperor, the empress—and Indy—joined him. Opening a leather dispatch case, Czernin produced a folded paper. Karl read through it, then handed the draft letter to Sixtus. The prince began reading, then stared at Czernin.

"This isn't what we talked about at all!" Sixtus protested, rattling the creamy parchment. "We spoke of guarantees, not platitudes and maybes."

"There is a language of diplomacy that must be employed," the count said quietly.

"To hell with your language, and to hell with your diplomacy!" Sixtus burst out.

"Let's just calm down," Karl soothed. "There's nothing to be gained by this."

Scowling, Sixtus sank into a chair. Karl took the letter. "Count Czernin, forgive my dear brother-in-law his rashness . . ."

The veteran diplomat's lips untightened a little.

". . . but I must agree, this letter is a bit more vague than I'd hoped," Karl went on.

"As it *must* be, Your Highness," Czernin said earnestly.

"But why?" Zita asked.

"One can't begin a negotiation by giving away the farm and all the livestock, can one?" Czernin pointed out. "More important, if the kaiser catches wind of what we're up to, we must have a fallback position."

"Fallback positions!" Sixtus surged to his feet again. "That's all you bloody diplomats care about, isn't it? Covering your rears!"

Czernin's face stayed as calm as ever, but Indy caught the flash in his eyes. "Young man, I am less concerned with 'covering my rear,' as you so vulgarly put it, than I am with covering the emperor's *back*!"

His voice hardly rose, but it was as if he'd cracked a whip. Silence filled the room.

The count turned to Karl, choosing his words carefully. "Your highness, I advise caution. I have been as explicit in this letter as I feel it is wise to be."

He reached into his morning coat, producing a pen. "It is now up to you whether or not you sign it."

Grim-faced, Karl looked from the paper to Count Czernin.

Indy held his breath. The emperor was supposed to be an absolute ruler. But Karl was just one man. And the most trusted member of his government was warning him of possible political disaster if the secret note was changed.

"I'm sure your advice is sound, Count," Karl said, taking the pen. "Though I still think this project was worthy of more risks."

Sighing deeply, he signed the diplomat's letter.

The mysterious Schultz (*right*) gives new Austrian identity papers to Indy, Prince Xavier, and Prince Sixtus.

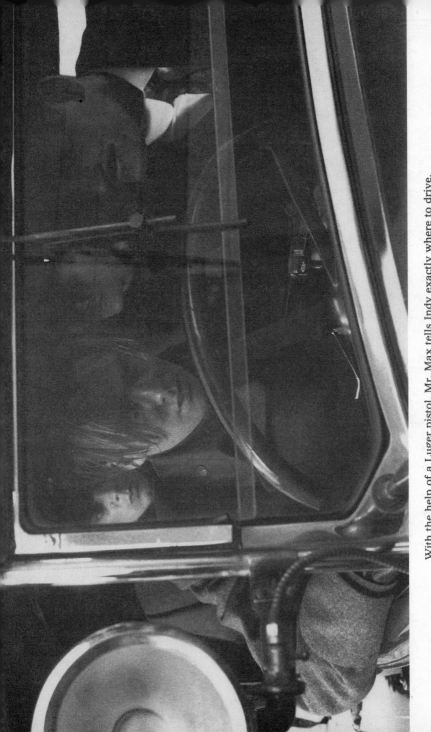

With the help of a Luger pistol, Mr. Max tells Indy exactly where to drive.

A frightening journey to an unknown destination outside Vienna ends in more terror for Indy and the princes.

Indy, the empress Zita, Count Czernin, Sixtus, and Xavier listen as the emperor Karl speaks of conditions for a secret peace.

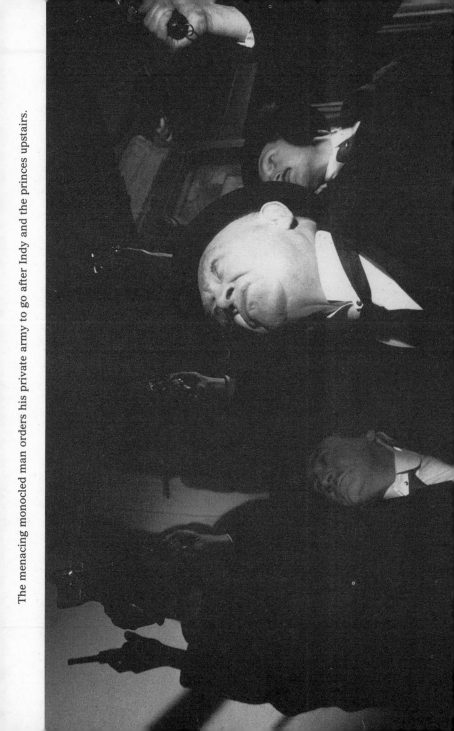

The menacing monocled man orders his private army to go after Indy and the princes upstairs.

Indy and the princes flee murderous thugs through the sinister alleyways of Vienna.

Disguised as secret agents, Sixtus and Xavier get past Count von Büler at the Austrian border.

In a daring move, Indy swings over the Swiss border to safety.

Chapter 9

Evening came, and Indy, Sixtus, and Xavier stood again in the courtyard of Laxenburg Castle. Once again they were dressed in their Austrian uniforms.

One of the trench-coated agents who'd led them here—the one with acne scars—handed Indy a slip of paper. "Go straight to this address," he said. "Mr. Max is waiting for you with new papers and civilian clothes for the return trip."

The agent stepped respectfully back as Karl

and Zita came up to make their farewells to Sixtus and Xavier. Behind them, Indy saw a line of cloaked palace guards. Also standing in the first rank was Count Czernin, watching the good-byes carefully.

"You have Count Czernin's letter in a safe place?" Karl asked.

Xavier patted his pocket. Karl gave him a hearty slap on the back. Then Zita gave him a hug. She and Karl moved on to Sixtus.

"I'm sorry if I embarrassed you," the older prince said.

"You could never embarrass us," Zita said warmly, giving him a farewell embrace. "Get home safely."

Karl now stood in front of Indy. "As for you, Captain, we won't forget all you've done for us." He flung his arms around Indy, catching him by surprise. "My brothers are precious to us. I know you'll take good care of them."

Indy was even more surprised to find a hand slipping something—an *envelope?*—into an inside pocket of his tunic. If Karl hadn't been an emperor, he could have found work as a magician, Indy thought.

The two exchanged a conspiratorial smile, and

Karl clapped him heartily on the back. Sixtus and Xavier climbed into the rear of the nondescript car that had taken them to the castle, and Indy slid behind the wheel. With a little further waving, they were on their way out of the castle grounds.

Sixtus sat slumped in his seat, finally leaning forward to glare at Indy as he drove down the road to Vienna.

"What are you looking so pleased about?" the older prince demanded. "This whole damn trip's wasted. That letter is worthless."

Indy's smile grew wider. "I have a feeling *this* one isn't." He pulled out the letter Karl had slipped into his pocket.

Sixtus snatched it, beginning to read. "To the French, British, and Belgian governments." His voice quickened. "I, His Imperial Majesty Emperor Karl of Austria-Hungary, do hereby sue for peace, in return for which I am willing to grant the following concessions . . ."

The car rang with laughter as they headed back to Vienna. No one noticed the black late-model Benz touring car that followed them all the way to town.

Heavy fog filled the streets of the city, dimming streetlights, blurring the buildings. Indy brought the car to a stop, peering through the gloom for the address they'd been given.

The street they rolled along was lined with big, featureless apartment buildings, less like homes than warehouses for people. Condensation gleamed on the cobblestones and sweated out of the building walls. "Not a person to be seen," Indy said. "Well, I guess that's better for us. Less witnesses to say we were here."

And less chance of getting stabbed by some passing thug, he added to himself.

He brought the car to a stop in front of the apartment block with the address they wanted. Indy and the princes got out.

They stepped into the shabby lobby, which was lit with a single dim light bulb. Indy led the way up a sickeningly creaky stairway that spiraled up at a steep angle. Indy's head was almost spinning as they finally reached their destination. Why is it, he wondered, that all spies have to live on top floors?

The hallway leading to Mr. Max's place was dark; only a few beams of light rose from the lobby below. Indy looked back at the princes. Weird, twisted shadows from the banisters turned their faces into grotesque masks. "Here's the apartment," Indy whispered.

He stepped to the warped wooden door and tapped quietly. There was no answer. Indy decided to knock a little harder. The door swung in on creaking hinges.

The dark apartment was shrouded in shadows. "Mr. Max?" Indy whispered. "Hello?" He felt around for a light switch, found one, and flicked it. No lights came on. All they heard was a rhythmic noise: *creak . . . creak . . . creak . . . creak . . .*

"What's that?" Sixtus whispered.

"There must be a light somewhere." Xavier poked his head in, looking around.

"Wait." Indy dug through his pockets. "I have matches." He found the box, removed a match, and flicked it with his thumbnail. The sudden glare of ignition blinded him for a second. Then Indy became aware of something dangling at eye level: a pair of shoes.

He and the princes looked up, to find Mr. Max. The gaunt man hung from the wrecked lighting fixture, his face twisted, his eyes bulging, his tongue pushed out between blue lips. A rope stretched from the ruined light to a knot behind the dead man's ear. They couldn't see the noose—it had dug too deeply into the flesh of the spy's throat.

For a second, Sixtus, Xavier, and Indy froze, staring in horror. "I think we should go now," Indy whispered.

A figure moved out of the apartment's other room. In the shadows, it looked like a huge, misshapen animal. Then it resolved itself into a huge, misshapen man. A big, coarse face gave them a demonic grin. He was missing an ear, and white scar tissue gleamed in the match light—so did the blade of a knife.

"What's your hurry?" he asked in German.

Chapter 10

A wild cry echoed round the room as Indy shook the match out. He was one voice yelling, but Sixtus and Xavier chimed right in.

Indy charged for the doorway to the other room. He had to take care of that giant before they could escape. At least the guy couldn't use that knife accurately in the dark.

Halfway across the room, Indy collided with a table. His breath *whoofed* out and stars appeared in front of his eyes. The table overturned, and Indy tumbled to the floor. Next time

I leap into action, I must remember to make sure nothing's in the way, he told himself.

As he staggered to his feet, Indy heard sounds of fighting ahead of him. Feet scuffled on worn floorboards, and he heard the dull thud of a fist striking flesh. That brought a cry of pain, different from the previous grunts and heavy breathing.

"I've got it!" Sixtus yelled. "I've got the knife!"

Indy pulled out another match and flicked it into life. The sudden flame showed the two royal brothers wrestling the huge goon, who had dragged them halfway across the room. It also gleamed off the blade of the knife, which was lying on the floor.

But the giant's face still carried that disgusting grin. And Indy could see why. His match flame reflected off the barrel of a broom-handled Mauser automatic. The big man laughed like a maniac. "I've got the *gun!*"

Swell, Indy thought. I've just shown this character where he should shoot.

He hurriedly blew out the match and dove for it. He was just in time, as the giant began firing at the spot where he'd been. Five shots rang out in rapid succession, smashing out the windows inches over Indy's head.

He landed and rolled, trying to get his feet under him again. The only view of the room he got now was from the muzzle flashes of the gunfire. The big guy had moved to cut them off from the door. He whirled around, sending more bullets flying.

One flash showed Sixtus and Xavier scrambling to the floor. The bullet shattered a vase, sending a shower of fragments over the two princes.

Indy had been counting the gunshots. At the tenth, he knew the automatic's clip was empty. He charged for the big man, bent to catch him low. Indy's head rammed the giant right in the gut, smashing into him like a cannonball.

The Mauser clattered to the floor as the huge German agent bent at the waist, losing his breath. Together, he and Indy hurtled backward.

Pumping his arms desperately, the big man tried to regain his balance. He couldn't do it, though, and he and Indy hit the warped wooden door to the apartment with their combined weights. The door slammed open, exploding outward in a spray of decaying wood.

It hardly slowed the two of them down. Together they crashed into the banister of the spiral staircase. Indy bounced off, getting thrown flat by the impact.

His huge opponent wasn't as lucky. The railing caught him in the small of the back. He teetered backward, overbalancing. The big man's hands clutched despairingly at thin air—there was nothing to grasp.

One heel caught in the tail of his long overcoat. The man's other leg went up, and over he went.

As the big man disappeared over the railing, Sixtus and Xavier came dashing from Mr. Max's apartment. They hauled Indy to his feet as the sound of a horrible, dull impact echoed up the stairway.

Indy clung to the banister, staring downward in horror. The spiral staircase made a bizarre frame for the giant's still figure, sprawled out on the stained marble floor far below.

Below, a bull-necked man in a black leather overcoat charged through the entrance, skidding to a halt when he saw the dead man. His bullet head tilted back, the dim single bulb gleaming off the monocle he wore. Behind him, a crew of men in identical dark trench coats poured in.

Glaring upward, the monocled man pointed

at the three figures at the top of the stairs. "Kill them."

His private army produced Mausers and came pouring up the stairs.

Well, there's no getting out of here the way we came in, Indy thought. He glanced overhead. There was one more flight of stairs above them, obviously leading to the roof. "Come on," he said, grabbing the princes by their arms.

They caught the hint immediately, pounding up the steps. The door at the top was locked, but in as poor repair as the one that led to the late Mr. Max's lair. It tore outward as three shoulders hit it.

Indy staggered for a second, desperately searching for an escape route across the roof. He started off, leading the way through a rooftop obstacle course. Chimneys rose at unexpected intervals, and skylights abruptly appeared under their feet.

Indy and his friends found themselves dodging and veering, unable to keep to any sort of planned course. Behind them, the rooftop door tore open again as the horde of killers came piling out. Indy poured on an extra burst of speed . . .

. . . and came to a screeching halt as he realized he'd come to the roof's edge. This apartment building was one of those huge, fill-the-whole-block affairs. The nearest building was across an alleyway. The distance wasn't too wide . . . if they were kangaroos. But no human could leap that far.

"There they are!" a shout came from behind them.

Mausers snarled, and bullets tore into the tile and brickwork around them.

"Jump!" Indy yelled.

Crouched low to offer as small a target as possible, they flung themselves from the rooftop.

Chapter 11

Indy and the princes watched about five feet of slanted roof tiles fly past as they dropped. Then their fall was broken by the fire escape ten feet farther below.

They landed with a deafening crash, and the cast-iron structure shook alarmingly. For a horrible instant, Indy wondered if the blasted thing was going to tear loose and plunge them to the ground.

This is all we need, he thought. Instead of escaping, the three of us create an outdoor imitation of that big guy's swan dive.

But the metal held, and soon Indy, Sixtus, and Xavier were clattering down the cast-iron steps. Indy dropped to the next level, taking a second for a quick glance upward. The princes' faces were tight as they charged along.

By the time they reached the level below, however, their pursuers had arrived at the top. Gunshots split the night. A bullet *spang*ed off a metal strut inches from Indy's head, a fat spark leaping from the impact.

Indy increased his speed, the princes right at his heels. They reached the last level of the fire escape, hurtled over the cast-iron railing, and dropped to an alley below.

Indy and his friends hit the ground running. Got to make it round the corner of the next building, Indy told himself. Otherwise, we're sitting ducks down here.

They flung themselves around the corner as a Mauser bullet smashed a large chip of stone away. Sixtus sagged against the wall, breathing heavily. Indy seized his arm and pulled him along.

"Rest there," he gasped, "and those guys will be right beside you in a second."

They stumbled into a run again, dashing across a wide *Strasse* to a section of older houses and tiny, crooked alleys. Behind them, heavy hobnailed boots, clattering on cobblestones, charged in pursuit.

Indy had no time to think, no time to plan a course. He darted in this direction and that, threading his way through a maze of mist-filled alleys with only the occasional street lamp to show the way.

His feet skidded on a piece of ripe garbage at one turn, and Indy nearly flopped right on his face. It could be worse, he discovered. A couple of alleys later, Indy heard Xavier give a cry of disgust that didn't quite drown out the loud squeal from the rat he'd stepped on.

Pursuing footsteps pounded after them, never far behind, echoing off the stone-fronted buildings.

Indy paused at a two-way turning. Which way to go? He was completely disoriented by this constant runaround.

Wheezing, Xavier and Sixtus caught up to him. "This way!" Indy said, picking a route at random.

Breaking into a run again, they got about halfway down the alley before a pair of figures appeared at the opening ahead of them. Judging from the silhouettes of trench coats and slouch hats, they were twins to the killers pursuing them. Of course, Indy realized, there were also the distinctive outlines of the Mauser pistols dangling from the men's hands.

"Oops—wrong way!" Indy whipped round in mid-step, doubling back on his course with the princes right behind.

As they passed the intersection with the alley they'd just left, a cry of triumph echoed off the blank walls. Indy, Xavier, and Sixtus skittered around a blind corner as the two sets of pursuers joined forces behind them.

The death squad stormed down the alley, blood lust in their eyes. Their prey couldn't hope to escape now. There was no margin for escape. They were mere seconds behind. . . .

Hobnailed footfalls echoed off the walls of a much larger space, then stumbled to silence. The killers milled around in confusion. They'd burst out into an open square, a big expanse of cobblestones with nowhere to hide. So where were the people they'd been chasing?

More footsteps rang down the alleyway. Another squad of killers arrived, led by the bullet-headed man with the monocle. The eyepiece glittered almost as dangerously as his free eye while he glared around. "What happened?" he barked. "Where are they?"

The leader of the first group, a grim-looking type with an eyepatch, removed his slouch hat to scratch his close-cropped hair. "Count von Büler, we were right behind them!"

"We came right around the corner and they were gone!" another killer said sheepishly. "Vanished!"

The count looked as if he were about to explode with cursing and swearing. Then he suddenly stopped, looking downward.

A cat rubbed along his stylishly tailored ankle, purring. It raised a playful paw, tapping at the count's shoelaces.

His face tight with disgust, the count kicked the animal away. With a yowl, the cat skittered off.

"I want this square searched from one end to the other!" the count growled at his assembled troops. "Every nook and cranny, every bloody inch! I want them found!"

The group broke into search parties, splitting all over the square. Hissing, the cat watched them go. With a slinking gait, it headed away from these unpleasant humans.

Abruptly, the cat stopped at a manhole cover, sniffed, and meowed plaintively.

As the cat padded away, a sigh rose from under the manhole cover. . . .

Chapter 12

Indiana Jones stumbled along in pitch darkness. One hand slid along the slimy stone wall to his right. His other hand was flung over the lower half of his face, holding the handkerchief against his nose and mouth.

Behind him, a hand—Xavier's—gripped his shoulder, while Sixtus brought up the rear. The other two also had cloth over their faces.

Tears ran from Indy's eyes. These weren't from trying to pierce the impenetrable darkness, however. They came from the stink that rose from the walls, the floors, the water flowing off to one side—a smell that could be cut with a knife.

Yet it was the smell that made him unwilling to light any of his matches. Some kinds of sewer gas were flammable, even explosive. And here in the sewers of Vienna, Indy suspected that he and the princes had found the mother lode of those gases.

So instead, they scuffed blindly on along the slippery cobblestone flooring, their feet sliding on an unseen, oily, disgusting muck. In the darkness, Indy couldn't tell if they were in a huge open space or a tiny enclosed one. His ears were useless for detecting any clues—all they heard was the rush of water going past.

But the worst part of all was the smell, which struck them like a physical blow. It was the rancid rot of overripe garbage mixed with a sharp chemical reek, plus a foulness from things he didn't even want to think about. Visit Vienna, he thought bitterly, the stink capital of Europe.

Every once in a while, they passed a water collector or manhole. Then they could see their way for a few steps with the aid of street-lamp light filtering in through the openings. It could be worse, Indy told himself. At least they were on a railed walkway above the flow of filthy water.

"What awful bad luck," Xavier said as they walked along. "Of all the times for Mr. Max to be taken by the secret police, it had to be at our visit."

"Those people weren't the secret police," Indy said grimly. "At least, not the Austrian variety."

Xavier stopped dead in his tracks, nearly losing his grip on Indy's shoulder. "Whatever do you mean?" he asked.

"Yes." Sixtus's voice sounded tight with annoyance, tiredness, and fear. "Where do you come off saying—"

"Did you see the guns they were trying to use on us?" Indy interrupted. "They were Mausers—broom-handled Mausers. That big thug in Mr. Max's room got off ten shots."

"So?" Xavier asked impatiently.

"The Austrians use the Steyr automatic—*eight* shots," Indy told them. "And it's a much squarer gun than the Mauser." He took a deep breath, and immediately regretted it. "Those men chasing us weren't carrying Austrian guns, so I don't think they were Austrians."

"Wait a moment," Sixtus protested. "When

Mr. Max threatened you, he used a nine-milli-meter Parabellum. That's a German officer's gun, but you didn't think he was a German spy."

"Sure—he got hold of *one* Luger," Indy said. "Not too difficult, I think, in a city crawling with German officers. The thing is, the men who attacked us had their guns in bulk, like an army. And guess which country arms itself like that?"

"Germany," Xavier and Sixtus both said in quiet voices.

"So it looks as if the kaiser's boys know we're in town and may have an idea of what we're up to," Indy said. "We'll have to be more careful than ever if we expect to get out of here alive."

Indy's warning paid off pretty quickly. The princes urged him to get them out of this smelly hiding place as quickly as possible. But when Indy climbed the iron ladder to the next manhole, he heard voices in the distance. They weren't speaking in the softer, slurred accents of *Wienerisch*, Vienna's version of German. No, these voices spoke the harsher, curter accent of northern Germany.

Indy climbed back down to Sixtus and Xavier. "We keep walking underground," he told them. "They're still searching the streets above for us."

They trekked on for a long time through the sewers. At a couple of points, they even had to wade through streams of filthy water to switch to new routes. When Indy finally led the way up to street level, they were miles from where they'd gone underground.

Indy hurried the two princes along, however. They still had to get out of the city, and the easiest way would be one of the suburban railroad stations. Not until they were safely aboard a westbound train did Indy allow some rest.

Sixtus and Xavier took up one side of the train compartment in a very un-regal huddle. The princes lay almost unmoving, completely exhausted.

At long last, Sixtus managed to summon up enough energy to brush at his jacket. He sniffed and shook his head. "The sewer was a really wonderful idea. What an incredible smell you've discovered."

Xavier was lucky. Crossing the chilly sewer water had given him a cold. Whatever they smelled like, he couldn't tell. His nose was too stuffed.

He stifled a sneeze, then looked up in concern. "Wait a moment. How's the letter? Is it . . . ?"

Even the effort of raising a hand to check the inner pocket of his tunic was a struggle for Indy. "A bit damp," he announced. "But still intact."

A smile tugged at the corners of Xavier's lips. "Just like us."

For a second there was silence. Then, slowly, Sixtus began to chuckle. Indy joined in, then Xavier. It wasn't an all-out laugh, though. They were all too bone-weary for laughter.

Finally, however, the chuckling died down. Sixtus glanced down at the field-gray tunic he was wearing. "How can we hope to get across the border in these uniforms?" he asked worriedly. "We were supposed to get new papers, civilian clothes . . ."

Indy felt his eyes closing, in spite of his efforts to keep awake. "Don't worry," he told the prince. "I'll think of something. . . ."

Sunlight poured through the train compartment's open window. A cold breeze came in, too, but that was what the occupants had hoped for. They had to air out their sewer-tainted clothes.

Indy stretched limply across his seat, sprawled like a puppet with its strings cut. His head was thrown back, his mouth open in a deep sleep.

The princes were leaning together for warmth, snoring at the top of their lungs.

Even when the train lurched to a stop, they didn't rouse. Indy was flung forward by the jerk of the brakes; he straightened up a little and blinked, but was about to fall back asleep when the conductor passed their compartment door.

"Götzis!" the conductor bellowed in that cheerful "Great morning, isn't it?" way that conductors have at the crack of dawn. "All off for Götzis! Last stop before the Swiss border!"

That brought Indy fully awake. He leaned over to rouse the sleeping brothers. Then, blearily, he looked out the compartment window.

"Oh, no!" Indy's eyes were wide open now. His voice was hoarse.

Sixtus and Xavier looked out the window as well. They gasped as they recognized the heavyset figure standing at the rear of the crowd on the wooden station platform.

That nearly shaven, bullet head, that monocle, that expression like a wild beast that had just smelled blood—it was the man who'd led their deadly pursuit the night before!

Chapter 13

"How did he find us?" Sixtus gasped as he, Indy, and Xavier ducked desperately away from the window. They had pulled back just in time, Indy figured. His last look through the glass had shown another squad of cold-faced killers gathering around their boss.

The whole group advanced on the train, scanning the windows.

"They're probably checking every train out of Austria," Indy told the princes. "*Especially* the trains to Switzerland."

Sixtus and Xavier stared at Indy, half hopeful, half afraid of what he'd tell them.

Great, Indy told himself. They're depending on me to get them out of this. And I have no idea how to do that.

The train suddenly lurched forward again, leaving the station. "Mr. Monocle and his boys have probably just climbed aboard," Indy said to the two young men. "Most likely, they'll begin searching the train. That gives us two choices. We can stay here like rats in a trap, or we can get going."

Sixtus threw open the compartment door and they started down the corridor of the train carriage. "Okay," Indy muttered. "At least now we're a *moving* target."

"Look on the bright side," Xavier told him. "We're not leaving behind any luggage."

They reached the end of the carriage. With the caution born of too many chases on trains, Indy peered through the window of the connecting door, scanning the next car before they stepped through.

He was glad he had. Two figures in trench coats and slouch hats moved slowly down the corridor. They peered into every compartment they passed.

Indy hurriedly stepped back and shepherded the princes in the opposite direction. "They've split into pairs to search the train," he said quickly. "And they're right ahead of us."

Sixtus, Xavier, and Indy sped to the far side of their carriage. The princes squeezed into a recessed area by the doorway as Indy peered through.

"Bad news," he reported. "There's another pair of them in the *next* car. We're trapped."

He turned to regard the princes' pale faces, and noticed the lettering on the door their backs were pressed to. "DAMEN," he read aloud. "That's German for 'ladies.' " A grin tugged at his lips. "Are you game, gentlemen? It's our only hope."

They disappeared inside.

Two trained German assassins opened the door between train cars and stepped through. One held the door. The other kept his hand in the pocket of his trench coat, but the outline of the gun he held there was obvious. Count von Büler's orders had been specific. Search every space aboard the train for the three Allied spies in Austrian uniforms. Do it discreetly. Capture at least one of them alive.

The men had been trained to kill people in a

dozen ways. They could clear a jammed bullet from their Mauser pistols in a second. But at this part of the search, they paused. Nowhere in their training had there been any mention of searching ladies' rooms.

Slipping his gun out of hiding, Hans pushed the door open. He and Fritz poked their heads in.

"Hello?" Hans said tentatively.

His answer was a shriek like a steam whistle.

"Beast!" a high-pitched, quavering old voice shrieked at him. "How *dare* you come in here?"

Poor Hans blushed to the roots of his blond hair. He hurriedly thrust his pistol away.

Another strident, cackling voice came from the next-door stall. "Hildegarde! Call the conductor at once!"

Hans and Fritz exchanged worried glances. A *discreet* search, the count had told them. Silently, they shut the door and hurried down the corridor.

A moment after the door had slammed shut, Indy peered over the entrance to his stall. "One of my best disguises," he said with a grin.

A second later, Xavier and Sixtus were peering over their doors, too.

"We'll just—" Sixtus began in the same high-pitched cackle he'd just used. Embarrassed, he cleared his throat and started again in a normal tone. "We'll just have to jump off the train and try to cross the border on foot."

"We'll break our necks!" Xavier protested.

"I prefer that to being shot!" Sixtus replied.

"You still might wind up that way," Indy said. "Remember the fence at the border? The barbed wire? The guards with rifles?" He frowned, then a gleam came into his eyes. "No, wait. I have a better idea. . . ."

Hans and Fritz had made their way to the dining car. At the entrance, they found a conductor.

"We're looking for three Austrian soldiers." Hans's voice was a low-pitched, lethal murmur. "Deserters. Seen them?"

The conductor's eyes went from one trench-coated figure to the other. Secret police. They had to be. Sweat appeared on his brow. "I—I have seen nothing," he said, shaking his head.

The two German agents stepped past the nervous ticket-taker and into the dining car. There were a few people at the tables. One look at these grim figures and all conversation ceased.

At the far end of the car, the door flew open and in breezed Indiana Jones, still wearing his Austrian uniform. He was whistling a cheerful tune, and didn't seem aware of the silence until he'd gotten well into the room. When he saw the two agents, his whistling broke off.

"You!" Fritz shouted. "Stay there!"

Instead, Indy whirled around and bolted for the far door.

Hans and Fritz dashed down the center of the car. Indy grabbed the handle of the carriage door, then swung around, stretching out his other hand to the last table.

As Hans and Fritz came up, Indy whipped the tablecloth off. Saucers, coffee cups, and silverware went flying. The German agents got tangled in the billowing linen. Indy tore the door open and dashed down the corridor of the next car.

Quickly freeing themselves, Hans and Fritz clattered in pursuit. Both had now pulled out their Mausers.

Running down the corridor, Indy rapped sharply on the door of each compartment he passed. His timing was perfect. Just as Hans and Fritz arrived, curious passengers appeared in the corridor, responding to the knocks.

Ordered to be discreet, Hans and Fritz couldn't start shooting. As it was, women began screaming and children crying when they saw the guns. A fat, white-haired man stepped grumpily into the aisle, and they crashed into him.

"Get back inside! Quickly! *Schnell!* That is an order!" Hans barked.

These people knew about orders. They quickly left the corridor.

But Indy had already reached the far end of the carriage and gotten through the door.

Hans and Fritz plunged down the aisle after him, tore open the carriage door, and found their way blocked now by a solid wooden barrier.

"It's the baggage car!" Hans shouted, pushing against the door. It didn't give. "He must have jammed it shut!"

Pushing the muzzle of his Mauser at the wood around the handle, he began blasting. He hammered at the door, and it began to give way.

Acting together, Hans and Fritz took three steps back and hurled themselves against the weakened door. It resisted, but gave a little more.

The two killers shared a mirthless grin, stepped back, and put their shoulders to it again—and again. On their third try, the wooden door finally broke down. The two German agents were now inside the baggage car.

An irregular aisle threaded its way down the middle of the car. It zigzagged around crates, boxes, trunks, and piles of suitcases.

There should have been a million hiding places. But Indiana Jones stood pressed to the far wall of the baggage car, his back pressed to solid wood. There was no exit there.

Seeing Hans and Fritz, Indy sobbed. He sank to his knees, and tears appeared in his eyes.

"D-d-don't kill me!" he begged, his voice a desperate whine. *"Pleeeeeease!"*

Chapter 14

"So," Fritz said softly, starting down the baggage-car aisle. "The clever spy isn't so cocky now. He has run out of tricks, *ja*?"

"Don't worry, spy," Hans told Indy as he moved up beside his partner. "We won't kill you."

He laughed, but it was not a pleasant sound. "At least, we won't kill you until *after* Count von Büler questions you."

The splintery wood of the baggage-car wall rasped against the back of Indy's uniform jacket as he cowered. His wide eyes never left the Germans as they advanced. With every step, his sniveling and pleading got louder.

"Anything, I'll tell you anything you want. I'll give your count my code book. I'll identify other spies in Austria for him. Just—just spare my life."

Hans and Fritz came up to two big leather trunks. From there to where Indy groveled there was a clear space.

Indy clasped his hands together, blubbering. "B-b-believe me, I'll do anything. I'll give anything. I'll . . . *give it to them, boys!*"

The Germans had passed the trunks. Emerging from the concealing shadows, Sixtus and Xavier stepped behind them, wooden ax handles raised high.

Hans and Fritz stopped in surprise at Indy's yell just as the handles whacked into their skulls.

Fritz went down like a felled tree.

Hans, however, must have had a harder head. He frowned, glared at Indy, took another step, and began raising his gun. Then, like a balloon losing air, he sank to the floor.

Xavier stepped forward, his handle raised for another blow. But it wasn't needed. "He's out like a light," the younger prince reported. "Just took a little longer to penetrate."

"An excellent plan," Sixtus complimented Indy, and tossed away his ax handle.

"Let's get on to step two," Indy said. "Quick! Out of those uniforms!"

Sixtus and Xavier quickly removed their stained, torn uniforms. No longer did they look like the handsome young officers who had ridden into Vienna. These clothes had been rumpled, slept in, shot at, fought in, and dragged through a sewer. The princes were happy to get out of them.

Meanwhile, Indy was busily stripping Hans down to his skivvies. Xavier quickly climbed into the slightly baggy suit.

Sixtus began taking Fritz's things.

Indy read through the papers he'd found in the German agents' pockets. "Couldn't have planned it better. This is perfect," he said, folding the papers into two batches. "You've even got German diplomatic immunity. These'll get you across the border, no problem."

He handed one set of papers to each brother. Sixtus fingered his new identity documents, frowning. "But what about you? How will you get across?"

"Don't worry about me," Indy cut him off. He reached into his uniform tunic, drawing Emperor Karl's secret letter from the inside pocket. The heavy parchment notepaper was a little crumpled now, but otherwise intact.

"You might want to air this out a bit, to get the Eau de Sewer out of it," Indy said with a grin. Then his face got serious as he pressed the note into Sixtus's hand. "Just get this letter back to France!"

"But—" Xavier began.

"My job is to get you two—and that letter— to safety," Indy reminded him. "I think that splitting our forces at this moment is the best way to do it."

The two princes still hesitated, turning troubled eyes to him.

"Hey, who's the professional around here?" Indy demanded. "Now get going!"

Sixtus and Xavier were still reluctant, but they moved to the exit of the baggage car. There was nothing more they could say.

Indy gave them a cheery wave, then shut the cracked door behind them. As soon as he was alone, his eyes darted frantically around the carriage and its stacked luggage. Speeches like that are all fine and good to send people off, he told himself. But how *am* I going to get out of this trap?

Count von Büler was the first person off when the train reached the processing platform at the Swiss-Austrian border. With an arrogant wave of his hand, he called over the officer in charge. The man was a grizzled veteran captain, whose face had been deeply scarred by Russian shrapnel in the opening campaign of the war.

The captain's one good eye went wide as Von Büler flashed his documents. "How may we serve you, Herr Count?" the captain asked, standing a bit straighter. The soldiers and secret police at the border checkpoint saw this and immediately stood at attention.

"I have information that deserters and spies may be trying to escape," Von Büler told the officer.

He went on in a loud voice, describing the three men he'd pursued from the Vienna apartment building. The German spymaster was well practiced. By the time he was finished, anyone hearing would have been able to recognize Indy, Sixtus, and Xavier. "You will assist my agents in searching the train and apprehending these men." Von Büler didn't request any help. He ordered it.

The well-greased checkpoint machinery went into action. Soldiers herded the passengers off the train, and the crowd slowly formed into a line passing through the gate in the wall. This time the soldiers and secret police were especially careful in examining travel papers.

Von Büler stood off to one side, keenly gazing at every face in the crowd. His fleshy face was tight, and his teeth showed between his lips. The expression wasn't a smile—it was more like the look of a big predator that has smelled wounded prey.

Aboard the train, the four remaining German agents tore through the carriages, searching each compartment, nook, and cranny. Their guns were out. There was no more need to be discreet on an empty train.

Two of the agents had developed a working technique for searching the compartments. They burst in, guns drawn. One kicked the space under the seats, while his partner stepped onto the worn upholstery, poking his pistol into the luggage racks overhead.

"Hah!" the lower-level searcher yelled, tearing away a travel blanket that hung down to conceal what was under a compartment seat. He swore fluently when the space turned out to be empty. Catching the woolen blanket on the raised sight of his Mauser muzzle, he tore it in two and flung the pieces aside. "Where is this miserable *Ausländer*?"

They slammed the compartment door so hard the glass window broke.

Indy heard the smashing and swearing. It came from directly below him. He rested his cheek against the soot-grimed roof of the train car, trying to keep as low as he could. The front of the locomotive was just a foot or two short of the border. If nobody spotted him from the platform . . . if the search team didn't climb up . . . if, if, if . . .

Indy watched as, below him, Sixtus and Xavier calmly slipped past Count von Büler. Their hats were pulled low, but that was the way most of the agents wore their headgear. Seeing the obvious secret policemen, the Austrian border guards were only too happy to stay out of their way and let them go wherever they wanted.

The two princes were showing their documents to the Swiss militiamen when a furious voice bawled, "Stop! Stop!"

Hans, the German agent whom Xavier had knocked out, staggered onto the train platform. He wore a baggy, dirty gray union suit, and had a hand pressed to the back of his head. His face was a brilliant red, partly from anger, Indy was sure, but also from embarrassment. A few women screamed at the unseemly display—what was this man up to, wandering about in his underwear?

Several people laughed.

But Count von Büler immediately recognized his agent. Pulling out his own Mauser, he shouted, *"Don't move that train!"*

From his hiding place, Indy saw Sixtus and Xavier taking advantage of the confusion. They retrieved their papers from the distracted Swiss border guards and crossed into Switzerland— and safety.

Indy stared at the feverish activity stirring around him. Rushing troops and secret-police agents swirled like a swarm of bees defending their hive.

The question was, Indy had to admit, could he make his move without getting stung?

Chapter 15

"It's all or nothing," Indy muttered through his teeth as he surged to his feet. He pelted along the roof of the railway carriage, running for the front of the train—and the safety of Switzerland.

Think of it as a hundred-yard dash—well, maybe a little more, he thought as he reached the end of the car. Indy didn't slow down, though. His legs pumped, he sprang . . .

. . . and landed heavily on the next car in line.

Okay, he thought, so maybe it's more like the hurdles.

"There he is!" Count von Büler's voice had all the blare of a bugle charge as he pointed upward from the railway platform. "You men inside! *Shoot through the roof!*"

Inside the train, the two remaining teams of German agents had met in the middle of a car. They stared at each other for a moment, baffled by the failure of their search; then they heard their leader's voice—and the pounding of footsteps overhead.

Like the well-trained killers they were, they reached into the heavy leather holsters under their trench coats. Out came the wooden rifle stocks, to be slammed in unison into the holding grooves in the backs of the pistol butts. In seconds, the agents had turned their pistols into carbines. Throwing the stocks to their shoulders, the men aimed at the ceiling and started blasting away.

Indy's running gait suddenly turned into a weird high-stepping dance as bullets started erupting around his feet. He zigzagged madly, trying to aim for where the people downstairs weren't shooting. And always, he kept pushing forward. If he could only get off this car . . .

"*Der Teufel!*" Count von Büler swore as Indy seemingly made it past the gauntlet of fire tearing through the train roof. He brought up his own Mauser, aiming to take the young spy in the head. . . .

Almost made it, Indy told himself. The end of the car was right in front of him. His only problem was that he'd have to run in a straight line to pick up enough speed for the leap. "Well, I won't get anyplace just standing here," he muttered.

Holding his breath, he took the last three steps.

The last killer in line heard the footsteps over his head, whirled, and fired a parting shot. His bullet came up at an angle, clipping the heel of Indy's shoe just as he jumped.

Indy was staggered by the impact, and when he landed on the next car roof, he sprawled face forward.

It was a lucky fall. Three bullets tore through the spot where Indy's head would have been if he'd stayed upright. Down below, Von Büler swore and swung to aim his Mauser again.

Indy scrambled to his feet and ran on.

As Xavier and Sixtus watched in horror, the

Austrian captain yelled to his troops. The soldiers shouldered their rifles and began firing. Secret-police types whipped out their Steyr automatics to add to the storm of lead.

Indy took a flying leap into the coal car. He belly-flopped down onto the fuel pile, listening to the symphony of bullets *spanging* off the car's metal sides. The engineer and his stoker had bailed out of the locomotive cab to avoid getting shot, so Indy had the engine to himself.

He ducked into the cab, swung out the window on the far side from the troops, and climbed onto the front of the locomotive.

Most of the target practice suddenly stopped. Then Indy realized why. This was a steam engine, and the front of the locomotive was actually a huge boiler with steam under hundreds of pounds of pressure. If a bullet pierced the boiler wall, the whole thing would explode like an enormous bomb. And the Austrian soldiers weren't eager to get blown up along with some suspected spy.

But a few gunshots rang out, aimed by sharpshooters too confident—or too angry—to stop firing as Indy dodged his way onward.

The big brass bell rocked, clanging wildly, as

a slug smashed into it. Then there was only the smokestack—and beyond that, the huge metal spout that stuck out of the water tower.

The foot-thick pipe swung down from the tower to help recharge the steam engines of trains. But it also swung sideways, and Indy intended to use that fact to his advantage.

Ducking behind the smokestack as another bullet ricocheted off, he jumped from the nose of the locomotive.

Indy arced through the air, his arms open. He smashed into the side of the water spout, almost bounced off, but managed to cling to it.

And as he hoped, the impact swung the big metal pipe forward, around . . . and over the Swiss border.

Legs kicking wildly, Indy let go of the pipe to drop onto Swiss soil. The last of Von Büler's bullets plowed through the metal ductwork an instant too late.

The Swiss militiamen moved like clockwork. Their guns were leveled at Indy, with the *snick-clack* of bullets being fed into the rifle bolts.

Indy immediately raised his hands. "I surrender! I surrender!" he yelled. "I'm an Austrian deserter seeking asylum!"

Back on the Austrian side, Count von Büler

hurled his Mauser in the dust, glaring at Indy. All he could report to Berlin was that secret agents had seen the Austrian emperor. As to what they had discussed, he hadn't a clue.

On the Swiss side of the border, Sixtus and Xavier grinned broadly. As soon as they got to Geneva, they'd be able to start the diplomatic wheels moving to save Indy. Sixtus slipped the piece of parchment out of his pocket and waved it in triumph.

Indy grinned as the Swiss soldiers prepared to march him off.

I may be a prisoner of war, he thought to himself. But what these guys don't know is that the war is almost over.

Historical Note

Sad to say, Indy's thought at the end of this story was wrong. World War I dragged on until November 1918, and millions more people—soldiers and civilians—died.

World War I is very much a historical fact, one of the great disasters of the twentieth century. It was in this war that generals learned that tactics which had been successful for a hundred years no longer worked against modern weapons—like machine guns. Learning those lessons created appalling casualties. In some battles, total losses on both sides came to more than a million men.

Certainly, Europe's big loser in the "Great War" (as it was known before we had World War II) was Austria-Hungary. In 1914, this country was the second-largest empire in Europe, with a population of more than fifty million.

By 1919, the empire had been completely broken up. Some of its land went to Italy and Romania. Parts went to construct entire new nations—Yugoslavia, Poland, and Czechoslovakia. Hungary became a separate nation. And Austria, the seat of the old empire, shrank to a tiny country with only seven million inhabitants.

Why did this happen? The lands gathered in by the old imperial Habsburg family contained many nationalities—and they all wanted their own countries. When Austria lost the war, these countries-in-waiting seized their chances, with the help of the victorious Allies.

Emperor Karl I was a real person, who took the imperial crown in 1916 after his great-uncle, Franz Josef, died. Karl had fought in the war and saw the danger to his empire if the conflict dragged on. He, his wife, Zita, and their foreign minister, Count Czernin, tried several times to arrange a separate peace for Austria-Hungary.

The secret mission of Sixtus and Xavier of Bourbon-Parma is a historical fact. They did indeed come to Vienna—although not led by Indiana Jones. The princes also returned to France with what came to be known as the Sixtus letter. In this note, Karl wrote that he would accept the three Allied conditions for peace.

Unfortunately, international affairs had changed from the days of dynastic diplomacy. The new French prime minister, Clemenceau, revealed the contents of the letter without acting on them. Karl was called to a meeting with Kaiser Wilhelm at German military headquarters in Spa, Belgium. The result was a signed agreement to continue the war until Germany won. As we know from history, however, Germany did *not* win.

With the collapse of the empire, Karl and Zita were pushed from power. Their lives were even in danger, until Prince Sixtus persuaded the British government to extend protection to them.

Karl made several unsuccessful attempts to

regain his crown. He died, nearly penniless, in 1922.

Years later, Kurt von Schuschnigg, the last chancellor of Austria before the Nazis annexed that country in 1938, wrote this about Karl: "Whether he was a great monarch, was wisely advised at all times, did the right thing always, is not the question here. To recognise that he was thoroughly good, brave and honest, and a true Austrian who wanted the best, and in misfortune bore himself more worthily than many other men would have done is to assert the truth—and this truth has been suppressed far too long."

Empress Zita lived for seventy more years after losing her crown. For those who think of history as the story of those long gone, it's interesting to remember that this "historical figure" passed away only in 1989.

TO FIND OUT MORE . . .

Austria (Enchantment of the World series) by Carol Greene. Published by Childrens Press, 1986. A beautifully illustrated book about the history, culture, and geography of Austria. Perfect for researching a social studies paper, this book includes a handy "Mini-Facts at a Glance" section. Be sure to read the chapter on the Hapsburg family! As Xavier guessed, European royals probably *are* all related—thanks in no small part to the Hapsburgs' many strategic marriages. Color photographs, drawings, and maps.

An Album of World War I by Dorothy and Thomas Hoobler. Published by Franklin Watts, 1976. Packed with photographs and maps, this is an easy-to-read history of what was thought to be "the war to end all wars." Read about the assassination of Emperor Karl's uncle, the Archduke Franz Ferdinand—the shot that virtually started World War I. (And see the photographs taken moments before and after that incident!)

Triumphs and Tragedies in the East, 1915–1917 (The Military History of World War I series), Volume 4, by Trevor Nevitt Dupuy, Col., U.S. Army, Ret., and Wlodzimiez Onacewicz, Col., Polish Army, Ret. Published by Franklin Watts, 1967. With fascinating details, maps, and photographs galore, this book chronicles the struggles on the Eastern Front leading to the writing of the secret peace letter and to the ultimate decline and collapse of the Austro-Hungarian Empire. Photographs and maps.

The Master Book of Spies by Donald McCormick. Published by Franklin Watts, 1974. Into spy stories? Then chances are you'll love this book about the real world of international espionage. Gives an insider's view of the profession, from the how-tos of becoming a spy to the cat-and-mouse games nations play over captured spies. (Also includes a chapter on the classics of "spy literature"—and on how they're read by the pros to find new ideas and possible secret messages!) Photographs and drawings.

Cooking the Austrian Way (Easy Menu Ethnic Cookbooks series) by Helga Hughes. Lerner Publications Company, 1990. Satisfy your hunger for adventure—in your own kitchen! This collection of easy-to-follow recipes is filled with information about the history and dining customs of Austria. Learn how modern Austrian cuisine was influenced by foods from the different countries of the Austro-Hungarian Empire, and taste for yourself what Indy might have eaten had he visited Vienna during a more peaceful time.

7 - 27 - 92